Whiptail of Blackshale Trail

All inquiries should be addressed to:
Barron's Educational Series, Inc.
250 Wireless Boulevard
Hauppauge, NY 11788

International Standard Book Number 0-8120-1733-1

Library of Congress Catalog Card Number 93-13324

Library of Congress Cataloging-in-Publication Data

Foster, Kelli C.
  Whiptail of Blackshale Trail / by Foster & Erickson; illustrations by Kerri Gifford.
   p. cm.—(Get ready—get set—read!)
  Summary : An iguana tells two friends a spooky tale about a mysterious creature.
ISBN 0-8120-1733-1
   (1. Iguanas—Fiction.   2. Stories in rhyme.)
I. Erickson, Gina Clegg. II. Gifford, Kerri, ill. III. Title. IV. Series.
V. Series : Foster, Kelli C. Get ready—get set—read!
PZ8.3.F813Wh 1993
(E)—dc20   93-13324
                                                             CIP
                                                             AC

PRINTED IN HONG KONG
45   9927   98765432

GET READY...GET SET...READ!

Whiptail of Blackshale Trail

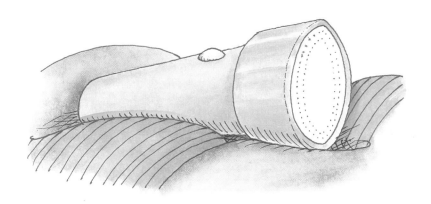

by
Foster & Erickson

Illustrations by
Kerri Gifford

BARRON'S

"Before you sleep,
let me tell you a tale

of the old Whiptail
of Blackshale Trail."

"Do you know this tale?"

"I don't," said Gail.
"Not me," said Dale.

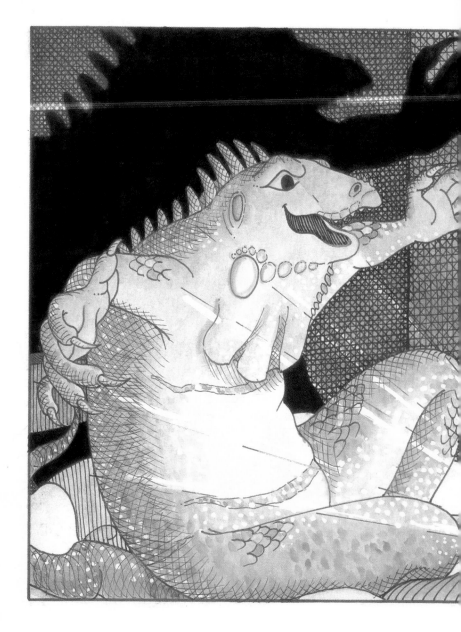

"The Whiptail is big,
with pale green scales.
Have you seen him?"

"No, never," said Gail.
"Not ever," said Dale.

"His eyes are as yellow
as Gail's pigtail.
Have you seen him?"

"No," said Gail.
"Not me," said Dale.

"His nails are long!
He can jump! He can sail!"

Gail and Dale went pale.

"His tail is long
and as fast as a whip.
Have you seen him?"

"No, never!" they wail.

"One last thing...

the Whiptail of
Blackshale Trail...

is sitting next
to Gail and Dale!"

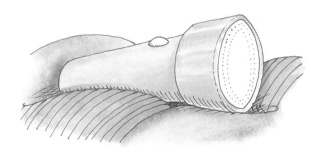

THE END

The ALE Word Family

Blackshale
Dale
pale
tale
scales

The AIL Word Family

Gail
Gail's
nails
sail
tail
trail
pigtail
wail

Sight Words

old
one
don't
ever
eyes
know
next
green
never
sleep
before
yellow
sitting

Dear Parents and Educators:

Welcome to *Get Ready...Get Set...Read!*

We've created these books to introduce children to the magic of reading.

Each story in the series is built around one or two word families. For example, *A Mop for Pop* uses the OP word family. Letters and letter blends are added to OP to form words such as TOP, LOP, and STOP. As you can see, once children are able to read OP, it is a simple task for them to read the entire word family. In addition to word families, we have used a limited number of "sight words." These are words found to occur with high frequency in books your child will soon be reading. Being able to identify sight words greatly increases reading skill.

You might find the steps outlined on the facing page useful in guiding your work with your beginning reader.

We had great fun creating these books, and great pleasure sharing them with our children. We hope *Get Ready...Get Set...Read!* helps make this first step in reading fun for you and your new reader.

Kelli C. Foster, PhD
Educational Psychologist

Gina Clegg Erickson, MA
Reading Specialist

Guidelines for Using *Get Ready...Get Set...Read!*

Step 1.   Read the story to your child.

Step 2.   Have your child read the Word Family list aloud several times.

Step 3.   Invent new words for the list. Print each new combination for your child to read. Remember, nonsense words can be used (*dat, kat, gat*).

Step 4.   Read the story *with* your child. He or she reads all of the Word Family words; you read the rest.

Step 5.   Have your child read the Sight Word list aloud several times.

Step 6.   Read the story *with* your child again. This time he or she reads the words from both lists; you read the rest.

Step 7.   Your child reads the entire book to you!

Titles in the
Get Ready...Get Set...Read! Series

30